T0247019

EDGAR
& ADOLF

PHIL EARLE & MICHAEL WAGG

OXFORD
UNIVERSITY PRESS

Barrington Stoke

Great Clarendon Street, Oxford, OX2 6DP, United Kingdom

Oxford University Press is a department of the University of Oxford.

It furthers the University's objective of excellence in research, scholarship, and education by publishing worldwide. Oxford is a registered trade mark of Oxford University Press in the UK and in certain other countries

British Library Cataloguing in Publication Data

Data available

ISBN 978-1-38-205550-5

1 3 5 7 9 10 8 6 4 2

Paper used in the production of this book is a natural, recyclable product made from wood grown in sustainable forests.

The manufacturing process conforms to the environmental regulations of the country of origin.

Printed in China by Golden Cup

Acknowledgements

Cover illustration by Tom Clohosy Cole

Emblems used with permission

The publisher would like to thank David Grant for writing the additional resources.

For Burto, a true and brilliant friend – PE

To Jan. And in memory of Mishi – MW

Edgar & Adolf *is a fictional story,*
inspired by real lives.

1

Scotland, 1983

Adi steps from the train on to the station platform. He's seventeen and feels a long way from Germany, his home. This may only be Scotland, but he feels like he could be on the moon.

The first thing Adi does is check his pocket. The small metal pin badge is there, safe. It hasn't fallen out. His mission is still on.

The train pulls away, groaning as it leaves. Then there is silence, broken only by the occasional chatter of a bird.

Adi has no idea where he is going, but he is relieved to see that the village is small. It should make things easier for him.

He walks from the station and starts to look around for something that might give him a clue about where the man lives. Adi's not sure what he's *actually* looking for: a football scarf in the window, a trophy on a shelf maybe?

But there are no clues anywhere. If this is a place where football is popular, then the people here do not shout about it. In fact, there are no shouts about anything. The village is quiet, which makes Adi feel nervous. What if he can't find who he is looking for? What happens if he fails?

Adi sees a park with two rusty swings, a tennis court with potholes in it, and a football pitch where the grass is too long for a proper passing game. A bunch of teenagers are on the pitch. They eye Adi as he nears.

"I am looking for someone," he tells them.

They shrug and stare. One of the teenagers comments that Adi sounds weird.

Adi tells them the man's name, Edgar Kail, and asks, "Do you know him?"

The teenagers don't answer. One of them makes fun of Adi's German accent.

But Adi isn't put off. He has travelled too far to give up now.

"The man I look for, he is English," Adi says. "So he will sound different too, like me. But not so *weird*."

Adi hopes his attempt at humour will make the teenagers want to help him. But the teenagers simply shake their heads. One of them asks Adi for a cigarette in an accent that is difficult for him to understand.

"This man I look for," Adi goes on. "He is a famous footballer. He *was* a famous footballer."

Surely this will help, he hopes.

But all they do is laugh. As Adi trudges off, he hears the teenagers mocking his accent again.

He walks on. He sees people on the street every few minutes and plucks up the courage to ask if they know Edgar Kail. But they all shake their heads. If they do know who Edgar Kail is, they don't want to tell Adi.

All Adi can do is keep searching. He looks for any sign or clue on every street. He wonders if it would be easier to knock on all the doors in the village, but how long would that take him? And has he got the courage to do it?

Adi might have no choice but to try every door. At least that way he'll know he's done all he can, even if he fails.

On a street corner, Adi spots a sign. There's a shop with the words *Post Office* painted on the window. He remembers these words from his

English oral exam. If anyone might know where Edgar Kail lives, it will be the people here.

The conversation Adi has in the Post Office is brief. Yes, they know the name Edgar Kail and explain the way to his house. But they say that Edgar hasn't been seen for a while. He's old. He may not have survived the winter. At least, that's what Adi thinks he heard. The accent here is so strong he can't be sure.

Adi walks faster as he nears the address. The final whistle is upon him. In the next few minutes he will either succeed or fail in his mission. Adi hasn't allowed himself to think about what he will do if he fails.

2

Adi finds the house. It is small – a cottage. Paint clings to the walls in places, but in others it has long given up.

He checks his pocket again, feels the precious badge sitting there.

He takes a deep breath and knocks on the door.

There is no reply.

Adi knocks once more, remembering Edgar Kail is old. He may be slow on his feet. He may be deaf. Adi waits, then tries again with a louder knock, but not an angry one.

There's a noise from inside – something falling to the floor. Then a single word. Adi doesn't know what it means but guesses it is a swear word.

The door opens slowly, and Adi stands straighter, as if he's about to meet royalty.

The man looking at Adi is old. His face is creased by time, his legs stiff. Adi looks for the strings that are holding this man up, as if he is an ancient puppet.

"What do you want?" the old man growls. He's not friendly at all, but Adi doesn't mind.

"I said, what do you want?" the old man says again. "Because if you're selling something, I don't want it. Do you hear me? Sling your hook!"

Adi doesn't move. He has nothing to sell. He wants to tell the man that he has been looking for him and how pleased he is to find him, but he's worried he won't say it right. So instead Adi says, "Herr Kail?"

The old man's face softens a bit.

"Are you German?" he asks.

"*Ja*. I mean, yes," Adi says.

"Long way to come," the old man replies. "Like I said, whatever you're selling, I don't want it!"

He goes to shut the door. Adi panics. He's sure this man is the person he has been looking for, and he can't let him get away. Not now.

"Herr Kail, I am not selling anything," Adi says before the door shuts. "And I do not want to disturb you. I bring you something. Something that belongs to you."

Adi can see that the old man doesn't know what he is talking about. He might think Adi is dangerous – that he wants to rob him. The old man tightens the scarf around his neck.

Adi reaches into his pocket, pulling out the small badge. He has carried it a long way, across the sea, from his home in Germany.

"Please, Herr Kail. Please?" Adi says. He reaches towards the old man's hand and lifts it up gently when Edgar seems reluctant.

Their palms touch as Adi passes the badge to the old man. It's so small that Edgar has to screw up his already wrinkly eyes to see what he is holding. When Edgar recognises it, his pupils widen and he looks at Adi differently.

The rusty old metal pin badge has a pink and blue crest on it, plus the words *Dulwich Hamlet FC* – they're faint but still readable.

Adi watches Edgar. The old man has a look of disbelief on his face. He doesn't understand how or why Adi has the badge. But he opens the door wider.

"You'd better come in," the old man says, and Adi follows him inside the house.

3

The old man's living room is dark, given that it's light outside. The curtains are half closed and dust dances in the light that has fought through the gap.

Adi looks around. The furniture is old, like the man in front of him. A chair has lost a leg and is propped up by an untidy pile of books.

Adi tries to work out how the room makes him feel, but the only word that comes to him is sad, which is not what he expected to feel. Not when he has finally managed to track down the person he has been searching for.

"So," says Edgar, his voice pulling Adi back to the present. The old man sounds cross again, like he did at the door. "Where did you get this? Because I know it isn't yours. It was mine, but I haven't seen it for more than forty years." Edgar is holding the rusty badge between them, his eyes narrow.

Adi has practised this moment many times in his head ever since he decided to go on this mission. He has a script, in both German and English, but as he stands here he doesn't feel like he can explain clearly. It's as if his script is now written in a language that Adi doesn't speak.

But Edgar is not in a patient mood.

"Is it money you're after?" he asks Adi. "Well, if it is, then you've come to the wrong place. You can look down the back of the sofa if you like, but you'll find nothing there except dust and sweet wrappers."

"Please, Herr Kail." Adi holds his hands up in a peaceful way. "The badge – it was given to me by my father."

"Was it now?" Edgar says. Adi can see he does not look convinced.

"Please, I explain," Adi goes on. "My father was given it by his own father."

"Your grandfather?" Edgar says, frowning. "What does he have to do with it?"

"You know him. My grandfather's name was ... Adolf Jäger."

Edgar's suspicious expression vanishes, and he gasps.

Adi sees Edgar's shock. He sees the old man's eyes widen. Adi didn't realise a name, two words, could make a person look so startled.

He watches Edgar's eyes go to the badge and widen further. His mouth moves, but no words come out.

"Please, Herr Kail," Adi begins to say as he sees the change in the old man's face. "I try to explain, if you will let me."

Edgar shuffles backwards, confused, until he feels the chair with three legs behind him. He sits, looks at Adi and waits to hear what he is about to say.

Adi rummages to find something in his bag. He's looking for a large plastic envelope packed full of old papers.

"Where is it?" Adi says as he searches, panicking that he cannot find what he needs. "Ah, yes. Here. This letter was given to my father by Adolf many, many years ago. But my father was not able to follow Adolf's wishes in the letter. Germany after the war was a difficult place to live for a long, long time. There was so much to rebuild, but also a lot of shame about what had happened. It is different for me now. And when my father passed this letter to me, I knew I must come to find you. So here I am. Please. Please read."

Adi hands a single sheet of yellowed paper to Edgar. The old man stares at the faded words on the page, his head shaking as well as his hands.

"I'm sorry," Edgar says, "but I don't speak German."

Adi feels embarrassed. Of course he can't. How stupid of him not to realise this. He moves closer to the old man and tries to explain.

"This letter was written by my grandfather when World War Two had started. It was attached to his will. Forgive me my English, but I think the letter says:

This is my final request, but it is very
important to me. If I do not live past
the war, I have something that needs
returning. A badge. A small pink and
blue pin badge. It was given to me by my
friend, a Dulwich Hamlet footballer called
Edgar Kail. The last time I saw my friend,
we swapped badges and promised to meet
after the war was over so we could give
them back. You will find his address at the
bottom of this letter, though I do not know

whether his house will still be there after
all this madness ends.

If the house is not there, go to Dulwich
Hamlet Football Club. Speak to the fans.
They will know where to find Edgar, as
he is their hero. The fans sing for him
at every game, about Edgar Kail being in
their hearts. It is a wonderful song. I find
myself singing it even now, years after
hearing it last.

You will find the badge in one of two
places. It is attached to my wallet or to the
clothes in which I died. I have carried it
with me ever since the day Edgar lent it to
me.

When you find Edgar, please let him
know I carry it always, even now. Please
also tell him how much his friendship
means to me.

As Adi finishes reading, he feels his hands shake.
But he calms down when he looks at Edgar. Gone
is his anger and his narrow eyes. Edgar's eyes look
tired and red, but they are also gently smiling, like
the rest of his face.

"Herr Kail?" Adi says.

"Please," says the old man. "Call me Edgar."

"Edgar." Adi likes how the word feels on his lips. "You look … happy now."

"Well, that's the effect your granddad had on people," Edgar says. "Adolf was a very special man. On and off the pitch. Clever and skilful. He was kind to me from the very first time we met. Not that I knew who Adolf was when I first laid eyes on him …"

Adi watches as Edgar leans forward. He blows into his hands to warm them before beginning to speak …

4

The Altona Stadium, Hamburg, 9 April 1925

The football ground was empty, but two of the four floodlights were on, giving the penalty box an icy glare.

Young Edgar Kail blew warm air into his cupped fists, but it hardly helped. His hands remained cold.

"Thank you, Herr Stöver," Edgar said to the groundsman, who had turned the lights on despite clearly not wanting to.

"Is fine," Stöver barked. "You are our guests. I am told to be nice."

Edgar bowed slightly to thank him, but to be honest, all he wanted to do was get running, to put some warmth in his bones.

"Your kit," the groundsman said. "It is strange. The colour." He made a face. A grimace.

Edgar looked at his jersey, unsure what was wrong with it.

"Pink and blue?" he said. "They're the best colours in the world, these. Perhaps I could get you one. As a thank you?"

Stöver waved his hands vigorously. "No, no, please. Thank you. No." He waved Edgar onto the pitch and stepped back into the shadows to watch.

Edgar didn't give the colour of his kit another second's thought. The pink and blue had always been in his life, for as long as he could remember. He wore a pink and blue scarf as a child on the terraces. The jersey he wore as a youth player had the same colours; then there was the scary, exciting time he first pulled on the kit and stepped over the white line at Dulwich Hamlet's ground, Champion Hill.

That excitement and the nerves never went away. That was why he was here at the football stadium and not with the other Hamlet players.

There had been plenty of chat at the hotel about what the team should do. Hamburg had a lot to offer. Art galleries, the docks, bars with beer glasses so huge you could curl up and sleep in them. But none of this held any interest for Edgar.

"You go," he said to his team-mates. "Enjoy yourselves. I'll go sightseeing after the match. I'm tired. Long day."

They'd laughed at Edgar of course, offering to make him hot milk and tuck him in before they left. He'd taken their wind-ups and waited until the echo of their footsteps had disappeared, then pulled on his kit and jogged to the stadium in the rain, ready to practise his crossing.

With Stöver watching, Edgar sprinted for two minutes, soon forgetting all about the cold and the rain. As he stepped into the floodlit half of the pitch, Edgar felt the buzz of excitement he got every time he played for his Hamlet. He was seventeen years old and every game was his biggest yet. Edgar had to make sure he was ready for the match tomorrow.

And so he began, swinging in a cross from the right, which dropped sweetly between the penalty spot and the six-yard line.

The only problem with the drill was that Edgar had just one ball, so after each cross he was forced to jog to the other side and dribble it back again. The leather ball was also growing heavier in the wet, testing his skill.

But Edgar didn't let that get in his way, and he practised hard. Cross after sweet cross flew in with just the right pace and whip. Edgar allowed himself a smile as he pictured Hamlet's centre forward, big Sid Nicol, getting on the end of his crosses tomorrow.

But still he didn't stop. He wasn't satisfied and carried on. The grey sock on his right leg slipped down to his ankle.

There was silence apart from the *thwack* of each cross. Then silence again.

It was so quiet, most people would have heard the creak of the rusty gate at the south entrance, but Edgar was focusing so hard he didn't notice. Even if he *had* looked round, he wouldn't have been able to see another man walk through the gate and stand in the dark half of the pitch.

The man was at least ten years older than Edgar and was feeling a bit rusty – like that gate, which the groundsman was always promising to oil but never got round to. The man was here for a bit of practice too before tomorrow's match – shooting practice.

On Edgar went, cross and collect, cross and collect, criticising himself when he didn't deliver perfection, smiling a little when he landed three good crosses in a row.

When the fourth cross left Edgar's boot, something different happened. Something beautiful.

As the ball flew into the area, Edgar saw a figure dart from the shadows. It was another player, wearing a different kit. The man sprinted forwards, his black, white and red hooped shirt a blur of lines. Edgar watched as the player bent his run slightly to correct the timing and hit the edge of the box just as the ball arrived.

The figure leaped, pulled his neck back for power, and *Boom!* His forehead met the ball, somewhere between a kiss and a punch, and it rocketed into the roof of the empty net. It all happened in the blink of an eye.

Silence again.

Edgar stood still, his eyes wide. He pulled up his grey sock and looked at the newcomer. He was an older man. Ten, fifteen years older maybe. Without a hair on the top of his head. But he was some player. Edgar could tell from just that one header. The older man looked at Edgar, breathing deeply, then made a slight movement with his hands – a fast silent clap as if to say "very good".

Then he fetched the ball from the back of the net, threw it out to the right wing and returned to his starting point outside the box.

Edgar collected the ball and set himself to send in another cross. He whipped it in and the older man was already on his way, timing his run to hit the penalty spot at the perfect time. Edgar's cross was lower this time, but the man shuffled his feet and swept his right boot to send it screaming into the bottom corner. Again he fetched the ball and this time threw it back with a wink.

For the next twenty minutes they formed an unexpected but instinctive partnership – the young lad in pink and blue, and the older man who had appeared from nowhere. The cross to the perfect spot, the timed run followed by a header or volley, leaving the back of the net bulging. Fetch the ball, throw it back to the wing, go again. The cross came in, *BOOM!* Goal. Fetch the ball, throw it back. Not a word was spoken. Half the pitch in darkness.

It was like the older man knew exactly where Edgar was going to land each cross. And this excited Edgar – made him realise he was in the company of someone very special.

They continued until the cold and damp became too much for both of them and then headed towards the changing rooms. At the tunnel the older man held out a hand.

"Adolf Jäger," he said.

Edgar thrust his hand out as the penny dropped. So this was Jäger, the Altona striker! Edgar's team-mates had told him repeatedly that this was the danger man in tomorrow's match. Give him an inch and he'd score a hatful, they'd said, and Edgar had seen that tonight, first hand.

"Edgar Kail," he replied. Edgar felt suddenly slightly nervous, though he had no need to be. Adolf placed his other hand on top of Edgar's and shook it warmly.

"I know," said Adolf.

Edgar's heart raced. How did he know? How had Adolf even heard of him? He was just a kid.

"It is a shame you will not be crossing for me tomorrow," said Adolf.

Edgar looked down at the muddy touchline. In his head he agreed. Imagine the score, he thought, if they *were* on the same side?

They shook hands a second time and walked to their changing rooms on opposite sides of the tunnel. Edgar's mind turned again to the game tomorrow. The biggest game of his life so far.

5

Scotland, 1983

In the dark living room, Adi is on his feet after
hearing Edgar's story. He can't help himself. He is
excited.

"This is the first time I am hearing anything
real about my grandfather and football," Adi
says. "I never met before with anyone who played
against him. I wish I could have seen him, even
in training. All I have are old pictures. That's all.
My father could remember very little about him,
especially about his football career."

Adi glances again at the walls of the living
room. They are bare besides a photograph of
a woman at the seaside and an old-fashioned
painting of mountains.

"Where do you live, son?" Edgar asks Adi.

"In Hamburg. Near to the Altona stadium."

"Ah. And do you ever go to watch them play?"

"Yes!" Adi replies. "Always. Every week I watch Altona 93. Home and away. And sometimes I am dreaming there. I try to think what it was like when my grandfather played, but it is hard."

"It was a long time ago," Edgar says, half to himself.

"What was he like as a player?" Adi asks. "He scored a lot of goals, yes?"

"Hundreds. He was a goal machine. And he didn't take any prisoners." Edgar smiles. "Adolf was always one step ahead of the defender. Here." Edgar taps his head to show that "here" means in his brain.

"Later, your granddad told me something," Edgar goes on. "He said, 'The first yard is in the head.' Do you know what that means?"

"Yes, I think so," Adi says, but it is not true. He doesn't want to admit that he has no idea. "So my grandfather scored in that game, when you first played against each other? How many did he score?"

"It's a long time ago, but as I recall he did score, yes. Other people did too."

Edgar pushes himself slowly out of his chair, making that strange noise that old people make when they stand up or sit down. Dust flies out of the arms of the chair as he pushes down on them.

"Wait here," Edgar says.

He leaves the room and slowly climbs the stairs. Adi stands and stares out of the window. It feels a bit like a dream. He can't believe that he has found Edgar Kail here, in this village. So far from where his mission started back in Germany. Adi feels happy. But at the same time, he can also see how old and frail Edgar is, and he doesn't want to upset him or tire him out.

There's a shout from upstairs. Then a scratching sound on the floor. Adi's instinct is to go and help. But Edgar is already on his way downstairs, faster than Adi expects him to be.

"Dropped it, didn't I?" Edgar says. "Clumsy old fool."

He is carrying a shoebox. He puts it on the small table next to his chair and then lowers himself down with that same strange old-people noise. Edgar picks the shoebox up and wipes dust off the lid with his sleeve. He points to a stool by the fire and Adi sits down. Edgar spends a few seconds searching through what's inside, then pulls out a thin slip of paper. It's a yellowy colour and ripped at the edges. But it has no creases. The paper is cut from a newspaper.

"Can you read English?" Edgar asks Adi.

"Yes. We did English at school."

Edgar hands Adi the newspaper cutting. "Here then, read this. I think it might interest you. But ignore the headline. It's a bit over the top."

Adi starts to read ...

6

KAIL IS KING AS DULWICH DAZZLE

10 April 1925

Altona 93 1–4 Dulwich Hamlet (AFC Stadium)

Fans packed the AFC stadium in Hamburg to see one man play, but they left talking about another.

This is not to say that the man they'd come to see had a bad game. The Altona centre forward Adolf Jäger scored a goal that would have lit up any stage – a drilled half-volley from just inside the penalty area. It just so happened that Dulwich's Edgar Kail, a seventeen-year-old right winger, scored on three occasions, each goal bettering the one that went before.

His first came after thirteen minutes, at the end of a jinking run. The second at fifty-three minutes could not have been more different: a right-footed shot that troubled the net as much as it did keeper Meier. Kail's third goal displayed heart and strength not often seen in a player so young and thin. It came after 78 minutes, when every other player's socks were coated in Hamburg mud. It is fitting that Kail's socks remained the same grey they were at the start of the match. After all, every time the young star touched the ball, he seemed to float above the grass.

But Edgar Kail did more than just score goals. Every cross was accurate, setting up Nicol for the other Dulwich goal. Kail's work rate was matched only by Jäger, who ran for 90 minutes, every inch the leader he is known to be. The same could not be said for Jäger's Altona team-mates.

Indeed, the scoreline would have been very different had the young Kail been supplying the crosses for Jäger.

And so the Pink and Blues of Dulwich continue their German tour in a happy mood, while the supporters who arrived excited to see one player definitely left thinking about two.

Adolf Jäger.

And young Edgar Kail.

Attendance: 3,321

7

Scotland, 1983

Adi finishes reading the newspaper report and stares at Edgar. He can't quite believe that the young hero from this match is sitting only a metre away.

"Wow," Adi says. "You were the same age as me now: seventeen. And *you* were the man of the match. Three goals! What do you call that in English?"

"A hat-trick," Edgar replies.

"Oh." Adi feels embarrassed for asking such a stupid question. "In Germany we call it the same thing."

Edgar takes the newspaper clipping and puts it safely back in his shoebox.

Adi watches Edgar as he smiles a little. *What is that smile about?* Adi thinks. Maybe the story has dragged up a happy memory for the old man. Perhaps it was his first great game for Dulwich Hamlet. Adi doesn't have to wait long to find out.

"I was lucky that night," Edgar says to Adi modestly. "I managed to drift inside a few times and find space. The Altona defenders didn't have the best game. And the keeper wasn't very happy when I saw him afterwards. Meier, I think he was called? He looked like he'd been slapped in the face with a fish."

Adi laughs at the joke but doesn't understand it.

He wants to ask more about his grandfather, but somehow it doesn't feel right. Not when he is sat in front of someone who was such a legend to the fans of Dulwich. *Kail is King*, the article said. Maybe Edgar was as great a player as Adolf? Better even?

Adi needs to know more about Edgar. He needs to fit this man and his grandfather together, so he continues. "Was that your first time in Hamburg?"

"It was my first time anywhere," Edgar says. "I'd never been abroad, never even left London before. I was nervous."

"This is my first time away from Germany," Adi tells him. "I was nervous also when I got on the boat. I didn't know if I would be able to find you."

Edgar looks lost in his own thoughts, and Adi waits until he is ready to reply.

"I was excited about the trip," Edgar says finally. "I must've packed my case a dozen times. I was scared I'd forget something: my boots or my pads. I was just a kid. I was always forgetting something."

"A kid, but also the star player," Adi says. "The newspaper tells us so!"

Edgar shakes his head. "You know what papers are like – always making people into something they're not. No, don't you believe the headline. Your granddad was still the star that night. He was a leader, fearless. He just didn't get the right crosses. Best player on the pitch. And an absolute gentleman off it."

Edgar closes his eyes for a moment. Adi thinks he must be tired and wonders how long he can keep asking these questions. Does the old man really want to talk? Should Adi let him rest?

But then, just as he thinks Edgar is drifting off to sleep, he opens his eyes and speaks.

"I went to see Adolf you know, after the match. There was something I needed him to do."

Adi leans forward to listen, but instead of talking, Edgar suddenly raps his fist twice on the table beside his chair. As if he's knocking on a door …

8

The Altona Stadium, Hamburg, 10 April 1925 – after the match

Edgar knocked twice on the changing-room door. He was fresh from a cold bath and was wearing his suit. His hair was combed and he was clutching something behind his back. As he waited for someone to open the door, he wondered what the mood was like behind it, inside the Altona changing room. The German players probably wouldn't welcome visitors or autograph hunters, Edgar thought. He wondered if strong words had been exchanged, truths spoken about their performance, players blamed. Probably. There was certainly no noise coming from inside the changing room as he heard his knock bounce around the walls.

Edgar knocked again and waited nervously, thinking about the man he was there to see: Adolf Jäger. Would he be happy to speak to Edgar?

At last Edgar heard a noise, a groan, then the door opened sharply.

"*Was?*" barked a voice. The German for "what". It was Meier, the goalkeeper.

I'm probably the last person he wants to see, thought Edgar, *after putting three goals past him*. He attempted a smile anyway.

"*Ja. Was?*" said Meier again, meaning, "Yes. What?"

"Er, excuse me," Edgar mumbled, shyly. "Is Mr Jäger there, please?"

"Yes. He is. Adolf! ... It's always Adolf they want," Meier muttered to himself as he walked away, before turning back to add, "I would have saved that third goal of yours if it hadn't hit that bump!"

Adolf came to the door. He was bathed and suited, changed for work. And he was smoking.

"*Moin.*"

"Sorry?" Edgar said. He hadn't a clue what that word meant.

Adolf smiled and repeated, "*Moin.* It means hello here in Hamburg."

"Oh."

"Cigarette?"

"No, thank you, I don't smoke," Edgar replied. He hadn't expected to see the great Adolf Jäger puffing on a fag.

"Good," Adolf said with a smile. "You're a sportsman. But then so am I. Still, I think of it as advertising."

"For what?"

"My job. I own a cigarette shop. What can I do for you?"

Edgar thought about Adolf Jäger working in a shop. He couldn't imagine this hero doing any kind of work apart from football.

"Herr Jäger," Edgar said, offering him his hand. "I just wanted to say ... well played."

"Er ... well played to you, too," Adolf said.

Edgar could see that his opponent was surprised. He wanted to say that he admired how Adolf had controlled the pace of the game and worked so tirelessly. Edgar wanted to explain that there was a lot he could learn from him, but no words came out. He stood there tongue-tied.

So Adolf put Edgar out of his misery. "A hat-trick for you, eh? A good start to your career, yes?" Adolf sighed. "The truth is, we couldn't cope with you running, er … rings … round us."

Edgar blushed. "Thank you. But I thought your finish was top drawer."

"Ah. Yes. Top drawer," Adolf repeated slowly. "Such a strange phrase."

"It means—" Edgar started to explain, but Adolf cut him off.

"I know. My English is very good, yes?" Adolf then frowned and continued. "I should have scored more. And maybe I would have if *you* had been crossing the ball in for me."

"Thank you," said Edgar.

"But … still … we are on the wrong sides," Adolf added quickly, his smile fading. "Anyway, I should be moving. I have to get back to my shop."

Adolf went to close the door.

"Wait," Edgar said, and put a toe in the room. "Please. I wanted to ask if you'd sign this." And he held out the match ball that he'd been hiding behind his back.

Edgar hadn't let it out of his sight since the referee had given it to him at the final whistle. It had even joined him in the cold bath with the rest of the team, where it had been used for a game of head tennis.

"You want me to sign it?" Adolf said. "Are you joking? Forget it."

He went to shut the door again. But Edgar stopped him.

"No, Mr Jäger, please. I'm serious."

Adolf frowned again. "Look, you did the hat-trick. You are the one who should be signing the match ball."

Edgar looked at it and pointed. "I already did, but—"

"Well, keep it somewhere safe," Adolf went on. "One day it might be valuable."

Meier called out something in German from the back of the changing room and Edgar kept talking, faster now. This really mattered to him.

"Please, Mr Jäger. It was an honour to play against you today. And you scored the Altona goal. I'd like both of our names on the ball. Please."

Adolf thought for a moment, so Edgar went on.

"One name from each team. Dulwich and Altona. Our clubs were formed in the same year, you know? And you're the hero here, just like, well … I hope I can become something similar at Dulwich. One day."

Adolf took another drag on his cigarette and stared at the young player for what seemed to

Edgar like an age. "You're a good player," Adolf said at last. "And I think you are ... honest too. So, give it here."

Adolf took the ball from Edgar and smiled.

He began to scratch his name into the leather, looping the g of his surname in his own special way.

"Maybe," Adolf said. "Maybe the next time we meet ... we will still be on different sides but playing in a much bigger stadium."

Edgar was confused. Were Altona moving to a larger ground?

"Maybe," said Adolf, "we won't be wearing our beloved club crests next time ..." He tossed the ball back to Edgar. "But instead the colours of our countries."

And Adolf shut the door, leaving Edgar to stand there, daydreaming.

Me? he thought. *Play for England?* It was too much to take in. He was still just a young lad from Dulwich and an amateur at that. But then again, what harm did it do to dream just a little?

Edgar looked at the names on the ball and felt a twist in his stomach.

He liked the idea of it very much. To play for his country against Adolf. To win an England cap ...

9

Scotland, 1983

"A cap?" Adi asks Edgar, confused. "Why do you need a cap? To keep the sun out of your eyes?"

This tickles the old man. "Sun?" Edgar says. "During a wintry English football season? You might need to wear a balaclava, but not a cap. No, it's what happens here when you start a game for England. They call it 'getting a cap', and they give you one too. A real cloth cap."

Adi frowns. "How strange. Would you not like to get a medal instead? My grandfather won lots in his career. I have them now. They sit on the shelf in my bedroom at home."

"Well," says Edgar, "medals are OK. I have plenty of them upstairs. But a cap is something special. An English thing, I suppose. A bit like a nice cup of tea. Speaking of which, I'll put the kettle on. Would you like some?"

It seems to Adi that Edgar is more alive now than at any point since he arrived.

"Er, yes, please," Adi replies. What he wants to say is "no, thanks", but he knows everyone drinks tea here, and he doesn't want to seem rude.

Edgar lifts himself slowly out of the chair and shuffles to the kitchen.

"Can I help?" Adi shouts after him.

"No, thanks," comes the reply. "I drank German tea once but never twice."

Edgar comes back a few minutes later carrying a tray with two cups, a jug of milk and a teapot half covered by a strange tasselled hat. Adi stands and the old man puts the tray on the stool.

"Ta daaaa," Edgar says, waving his hand with a mock magician's flourish.

It takes Adi a moment or two to spot Edgar's joke.

The hat perched on the teapot is not a hat at all. It is a cap. A rich blue cloth cap, with silver trim and a tassel hanging from its crown.

"That," Edgar says with a smile, "is my first England cap. I told you it was better than a medal, didn't I? A medal can't keep your tea warm."

"That is what they give you?" Adi asks. "For playing for your country?" He knows he should try to look impressed, but in all honesty, he is just confused. This is such a strange country.

"I have three of them," the old man continues. "For games against Spain, Belgium and, the best one of all, Germany. That cap was my first one, which now has this new use as a tea cosy. Here, try it on."

Edgar places it on Adi's head, but Adi doesn't let it stay there for long. He feels a bit foolish and wants to hear more. He doesn't want a strange cap to get in the way.

"So you *did* play against each other again," Adi asks, "you and my grandfather? For your countries? For your caps?"

"We did. Seven years after the first match. Milk and sugar?"

"Er, yes, please," Adi replies. He doesn't know whether that's the right answer. "Where was the game played?"

Edgar's hand is shaking slightly as he pours the milk. Adi wonders if it is caused by his age or the memories of that match pouring back.

"Where?" Edgar says. "Where else could it be played but the biggest stage of all? Wembley."

The old man reaches into his shoebox and pulls from it two things: a match-day programme and another faded newspaper clipping.

"It was terrifying," Edgar admits as he hands them to the boy. "I mean, making your England debut was scary enough, but to make matters worse, they made me face the press."

10

Press Room, Wembley Stadium, 14 March 1932

There was nothing that got reporters more excited than an England versus Germany match at Wembley.

The fizz of flashbulbs proved that as three men strode through the crowd: Edgar Kail, Adolf Jäger and England trainer Herbert Chapman. Two of the men had been through this before. One of them had not, and Edgar Kail was nervous, scared even.

The reporters' questions started before they had even taken their seats, rattling out like machine-gun fire. Herbert Chapman held his hands up, not in surrender but to try to keep some kind of peace.

"Gentlemen, please, you'll all get your chance," Herbert said. "Herr Jäger, Mr Kail and I will be delighted to answer any questions you may have.

As long as it's about football. I don't think any of us will be able to tell you which horse is going to win the Grand National."

There was brief polite laughter, then the questions started again. All of them were aimed at Edgar and Adolf, who sat beside each other.

Edgar, Edgar? Most boys dream of making their England debut against Germany at Wembley, so how will you cope with the occasion? After all, there is a HUGE difference between playing at Champion Hill and Wembley Stadium.

FLASH *FLASH*

Edgar, will being the only amateur player in the England side affect you?

FLASH

Edgar, this has to be the biggest week of your life. An England cap AND your wedding day? Is it right you're marrying the daughter of the Dulwich Hamlet groundsman, Rene? And has she banned you from wearing your England cap on the big day?!

Edgar, you've not previously played with any of your England team-mates. How much time have you had to build up any kind of understanding with them?

FLASH *FLASH*

Edgar was bemused. This wasn't what football had been about before. It hadn't been about questions or expectations or caps. And why did they want to know about Rene?

An hour before a match Edgar was normally at his other job, as a salesman for a drinks company. He would cycle to the football ground trying to empty his head of all the orders he still had to finish.

It wasn't until Edgar pulled the pink and blue jersey on that his mind would finally clear. Wasn't until the first whistle that he'd feel truly at home.

And right now? Well, he was as far from home as he could possibly be.

Edgar knew that he'd answered the questions, and he couldn't have done a bad job as there'd been no laughter or groans coming back at him.

But could he remember what he'd said? No, he could not.

Did he feel confident as a result? No, he did not.

Could he even feel his own fingers as they dug into his thighs?

No, he couldn't feel a thing.

Adolf Jäger was more comfortable, however. His hands rested on the table between puffs on his cigarette, and there was no sweat on his bald head despite the heat of the lights and the number of questions.

Herr Jäger, as you come from a similar amateur background, what advice could you offer Edgar here?

FLASH *FLASH*

Adolf's answer was brief but polite, full of nothing but praise for Kail, but Edgar wasn't able to absorb his words. Instead he focused on picking up his glass of water without spilling it.

Adolf? You must now see the end of your career running towards you. Do you ever regret staying with Altona 93 for all of it? Are there other teams you wish you had played for?

Even this question didn't seem to bother Adolf. No one liked to be told they were getting older, but if he was in any way upset, he didn't show it. In fact, Adolf embraced the question, talking in broken but confident English of exactly what he brought to the team.

The contrast between the two players was clear, to Edgar at least. Adolf Jäger was calm while he was a mess. As the press conference came to an end and the two men rose for photographs, Edgar was pleased to take his opponent's hand – that way no one could see his own hand was shaking.

Flashbulbs popped again as the reporters dreamed up headlines, and the two men parted, making their way to their own team's changing room.

Any talking now would have to be done on the pitch, and all Edgar could do was hope that he did not lose his voice.

11

JÄGER HUNTS DOWN ENGLISH

15 March 1932

England 0–1 Germany
(Wembley Stadium)

There were handshakes at the end of the match, a fitting gesture in these peaceful times, but that did little to cheer up 80,000 home fans who left disappointed after a poor England performance on a windy night in north London.

Playing Edgar Kail will be seen as a foolish move by many. England trainer Herbert Chapman rates young Kail very highly, and this was his first cap as replacement for Dennis Gee. But tonight the part-time Dulwich Hamlet player looked out of his depth, showing none of the crossing skills he is best known for. Kail was substituted after 68 minutes.

The spotlight instead stayed firmly and brightly on the German captain, Adolf Jäger.

The sly, clever striker pounced with the only goal in the 37th minute, after a fine cross from Willi Rutz.

Receiving the ball just inside the box, Jäger dragged it between his own legs with the heel of his right boot and left his defender bathing in the mud. He then thumped a low shot past Harry Hibbs in the England goal. Such skills are too rare these days and fans of both sides should all enjoy watching Jäger while he is still playing this beautiful game.

There was little for England's Three Lions to roar about over the ninety minutes. And after this performance it may be some time before we see young

Kail pull on an England jersey again. He must instead return to Dulwich's pink and blue, and to his day job as a drinks salesman. Indeed, Kail may be better suited to selling drinks in the Wembley bar after the match.

Attendance: 78,125

12

Scotland, 1983

Adi lets the newspaper clipping rest on his knees as he takes in what he has read.

"It is not what I expected to happen," Adi admits.

"Me neither. Even now," says Edgar with a sigh.

"I thought you were going to score the winner." Adi smiles wistfully. "Or even better, that you *and* my grandfather scored and the game was a draw."

"I wish you could've seen Adolf play that night, son," says Edgar. "He was masterful."

Adi sits forward, wanting to hear it all.

"Adolf had so much time on the ball," Edgar goes on, "even when he was surrounded by defenders. Plus he controlled the game even when he wasn't in possession."

Adi frowns and asks, "How?"

"Because he dragged defenders with him. They were scared of what he'd do when he DID get hold of it, you see."

"But it must have been hard for you," Adi says. "To lose your first England game?"

Edgar smiles, but it is not a convincing one. "Oh, I hated losing, but that didn't change whether I was playing for England, Dulwich or in the park with mates. But I was embarrassed that night – about how I'd coped with the pressure. I should've done better. Much better."

Adi sees Edgar wince and spots that his hands are screwed into fists – Adi understands that the loss still hurts now, despite the match being decades ago.

"I do understand," Adi says. "I am not a legend like you, or my grandfather, but I know I do not like to lose. That is why I looked so hard for you. The thought of going home having failed my mission? I could not do that."

"And you should be proud," Edgar says, tapping Adi supportively on the knee. "Your granddad had the same determination. On the pitch, Adolf was always focused – he thought about nothing but winning the match. That night at Wembley, my concentration wasn't where it should have been."

"Really?" Adi says, surprised.

"Really." Again Edgar looks embarrassed. "And I regretted it, believe me. In fact, it would've been a lot worse if I hadn't talked to your granddad afterwards."

"You had time to talk?"

"We did," Edgar says. "And I'm glad we did. Without the advice your granddad gave me in the bar after the match, it's possible my life would've turned out very different indeed."

And Edgar talks on, with Adi leaning in intently, not wanting to miss a word.

13

Wembley Stadium players' bar, 15 March 1932 – one hour after the match

Edgar stood at the bar for a good ten minutes, failing to buy a drink. He was disappointed, tired and frustrated, not to mention thirsty.

Making your debut for England was meant to be a wonderful thing, with a fairy-tale ending like scoring a last-minute winner. But when Edgar had been substituted, people barely clapped.

Maybe he should stick to the day job and kick a ball about at the weekends just for fun, he thought. Perhaps he should give up the stupid idea of playing at the top level. He felt like a fish out of water here at Wembley, on the pitch and in the bar, but he needed a drink. Finally he managed to catch the barman's eye.

Edgar leaned forward to speak but was distracted by a tap on his shoulder. He turned, just for a second, and the barman walked past.

"Bad luck," said Adolf from behind him.

"Doesn't matter. I can wait," Edgar said.

"I meant in the game," Adolf said.

"Oh. No, it's not about luck. I just didn't play well tonight."

"It is frustrating when that happens," said Adolf, "but do not beat yourself up about it."

Edgar felt his shoulders relax, just a touch, despite doubting Adolf had ever played as badly as he had.

"Maybe my mind wasn't fully on the game," said Edgar, turning back, trying to get served again.

"What'll you have, Mr Jäger?" the barman asked, beaming.

It was as if Adolf always had the spotlight on him, on the pitch and off. But Edgar didn't mind – how could he after what he'd seen Adolf do out there?

Edgar turned back to Adolf and said, "You took your goal so well. And that turn! We were talking about it in the changing room. What do you call it?"

"Two beers," Adolf said to the barman, and gestured for Edgar to put his money away. "Ah, yes, I call that turn *Die Falle*. The Trap. Go one way, then flick it between your own legs. The defender is not able to turn fast enough. He is stuck like a rabbit in a trap."

"I'll have to try it," said Edgar.

"Do. Next time."

"If there is one."

"Like I said, do not punish yourself," Adolf told Edgar. "There will be a next time, another chance, I'm sure of it."

"Maybe," Edgar replied.

Adolf looked at Edgar carefully, then said, "What was on your mind then, if not the game?"

Edgar hesitated, not sure if he should say, whether it was the done thing. But as the drinks arrived, Edgar found himself blurting it out.

"I had an offer yesterday. To join a big club, a really big club."

Adolf took a gulp of his beer and grinned cheekily. "Who, Altona 93?" he asked.

Edgar smiled. "Er, no. Chelsea. I think their offer might have been on my mind. Put me off a bit. Still, it's no excuse. I just don't know what to do about it."

Adolf took another glug of beer, giving Edgar the chance to ask a question.

"Have *you* ever had an offer from another club? A big club like Chelsea?"

"Have I had offers?" Adolf said. "I've had more offers than you've had cold drinks!"

Edgar smiled at Adolf's mistake. "You mean 'hot dinners', don't you?"

"No." Adolf raised his glass. "Cheers! The big Hamburg club tried to poach me. Schalke too. I got a letter from Bayern München and a telegram from Turin."

"Turin – you mean Juventus?" Edgar said. "Wow. How did you turn them down? The money, the crowds? Was it a difficult decision?"

"For me, no. The only question I had to ask myself was this: do I want to wear the shirt of another team?" Adolf looked at Edgar seriously and added, "Or is the shirt of Altona 93 enough?" Adolf paused, then continued, "The answer for me was clear. No, I do not want another team's shirt against my chest. Altona, for me, is everything."

Adolf paused again, smiling to himself. "Do you want another drink?"

"No, thanks," Edgar said.

"Edgar, I played my first match for Altona, and I will play my last match for Altona. One club. Only one. What will *you* do?"

"I don't know," said Edgar. "It's not about the money. I'm happy playing football and working too. But I have to do the right thing. Rene, my fiancée, she thinks I should go for it and join Chelsea. I love Dulwich but ..."

"You must do what this is telling you." Adolf pointed to the cloth badge on the left of Edgar's training top.

"The England badge?" Edgar asked.

"No. What is behind it. Your heart. The thing that makes you tick."

"But there's so much I might miss out on if I stay at Dulwich. You know, like you missing out on playing for Bayern Munich or Juventus!"

"But, you see, I already have so much," Adolf interrupted. "I have my shop. I have my family. And I have nights like this. Why risk it all to play full time? Why give up my job, my security, when it could end in an instant? The football, I mean. One bad tackle, one lunge from a clumsy defender. One moment, my friend, and it could all be over."

Edgar thought for a moment, still with no clue about what decision to make. Then he turned back to Adolf to buy him a drink.

But the barman's mouth was already open as he called, "*Time, gentlemen, please! The bar is now closed!*"

14

Adi sits and thinks about what his grandfather said to Edgar in the Wembley bar. Every week, every day now, Adi reads about players moving from club to club, with big transfer fees and bigger and bigger wages. Hearing about his grandfather's loyalty to one club moves him. It reminds Adi how he feels about Altona. He could never support another team. Never! It makes him wish even more that he had met Adolf and talked to him like he is talking to Edgar now.

Adi is thirsty. Thirsty to hear more, but also for another drink. The tea is good, sweet, so he asks for another cup.

"We've run out," Edgar replies.

"Of tea?" Adi asks, but then worries that maybe Edgar is referring to something else. Maybe he's run out of time. And that worries him. Adi wants to hear more about his grandfather, about Edgar too. He wants to know what happened next. He looks to the old man, sees the rusty old badge balanced on the arm of the chair.

"We've run out of milk, that's all," Edgar replies. "Wasn't expecting a guest, was I? I don't suppose you'd come with me to the Co-op, would you? I've a few other things to get as well."

"Oh, of course. Yes." Adi is relieved.

"It's a steep hill down into the village," the old man explains, "and I'm not always that steady on my feet. Not like I used to be."

Adi stands and reaches out a hand to help Edgar up. The old man collects his coat and fumbles with his keys to lock the door.

They head off together, deep in their own thoughts for a moment. Adi wonders if Edgar is still thinking of Wembley Stadium and the chances he missed. But what Adi wants to know is, what happened next between Edgar and his grandfather. There has to be more, surely?

As Edgar and Adi pass the park, they hear the yells, groans and laughs of a kick-about in full swing. Edgar stops to catch his breath.

"Hills weren't always a problem for me, you know," Edgar says. "Do you know what the Dulwich Hamlet stadium is called?"

"Ha, yes, I do," Adi replies. "Champion Hill. I was there two days ago." Adi's forehead creases again. "But it is very flat there I think. Not a hill at all."

Edgar looks surprised and asks, "What? So you went to the stadium before coming here?"

"Yes, of course. After trying the address I had for your home, I asked the Dulwich supporters where I could find you."

"And did they know?" Edgar asks quietly.

"Well, they know where you lived while you were a player. Lordship Lane, they tell me, in Dulwich. They say you marry the daughter of the Champion Hill groundsman, who was Scottish, and that you worked for a Scottish drinks company. In the end I found out from older fans it was this village here I must go to. It is a long way from Dulwich."

"They were always a good bunch, the Dulwich fans," Edgar says. "The Rabble, they're known as."

Adi frowns, confused at the word, and Edgar goes on. "Did you see a game while you were there?"

"Yes, they were playing against Whyteleafe. It was 2–1 to Dulwich. I enjoyed it, but I did think the English play ... I think you call it the 'long-ball game'. The ball is always in the air. They lost six balls over the wall."

Edgar shakes his head. "It doesn't surprise me."

"And let me tell you, Herr Kail ... Edgar," Adi says. "The fans, they are still singing your name. They did it in the first half and again in the second."

Adi is embarrassed by the sound of his voice. He doesn't really know the tune and wouldn't be able to sing it properly even if he did. But he knows he has to try, croaking quietly in his German accent:

Edgar Kail in my heart, keep me Dulwich.
Edgar Kail in my heart I pray ...

Thwack! comes a sound, interrupting Adi. He and Edgar both turn their heads towards the rough pitch.

"*Watch out, Granddad!*" shouts one of the lads playing. The ball is flying right towards Edgar.

The old man sticks out a leg instinctively and at the right moment turns his ankle just enough to trap the ball perfectly and bring it to a stop. Dead.

The lads playing the game stand and stare. One of them claps.

Adi smiles. Edgar looks down at his feet.

They both know that nothing needs to be said. In that moment Edgar looks young again. A player with the ball at his feet and his life ahead of him. In that moment they are both the same age: seventeen.

Edgar clears his throat and says, "We'd better get to the shop. Kick the ball back, will you? I've not got the strength in my legs."

Adi is embarrassed again. He loves watching football, but he knows he's hopeless at playing it. And here he is standing next to a professional.

But he has to have a go, he has to try, and he manages to hit the ball with just enough power that it rolls very gently towards the goalmouth and the lads waiting. They clap their hands slowly, mocking him.

"Not bad," Edgar says.

Adi knows the old man's being kind.

"But I think," Edgar adds with a smile, "that you're a bit too old to be spotted by a big club now. I'm not sure you'll ever play for Chelsea."

They walk on.

"And did you?" Adi asks. "Did you sign for a big club? Did you play in games in Europe?"

"No," Edgar replies. "Your granddad's advice was so good, I took it. I told him – I wrote him a letter about it. It was an important letter, as it turns out. That letter meant I got to play abroad again, and against your granddad too."

Adi pulls the rucksack off his back, excited.

"I think I know about this!" He beams. "The letter you speak about! I have it here! I read it many times but never understood really what it means until now."

They've arrived outside the Co-op, where there's a bench. Edgar sits gingerly, looking amazed at what Adi has just said.

Adi opens his rucksack and pulls out the plastic envelope. He searches frantically and hands Edgar a small folded piece of paper, the creases ironed by time.

Edgar is wide-eyed to see it.

"I can't believe you have this!" the old man says. "I can't believe that I'm holding something I sent so long ago."

He sounds slightly out of breath, despite being already seated.

"Do you mind if we rest for a minute?" Edgar asks. "I'd like to read it."

"Of course," Adi replies happily, and he steps away from the bench. He wants to watch Edgar read the letter but can see that the old man wishes to be alone with his grandfather.

15

9 September 1937

Dear Adolf,

I hope you don't mind me getting in touch with you like this. As you read on, I'm sure you will realise that my skills at letter writing are no better than my tackling. Sorry!

I've just heard that you are going to retire from football, and the news has affected me so hugely that I needed to write to you about it.

I'm so happy for you and your family. Think about the stories you'll have to tell your children and grandchildren. Enough to fill a book!

But at the same time, I have to admit to feeling real sadness too that the game of football will say goodbye to one of its most loyal and brilliant players.

What you have done for Germany, and of course for Altona, is something that the rest of us can only dream of.

I'm not sure that you are aware of this, but the advice you gave me in the bar at Wembley has never left me. When Chelsea made me an offer, it tempted me, more than I can explain. But it confused me too – so much so that it affected everything I did on the pitch.

It was only speaking to you that helped me make up my mind. Yes, of course I could move to a bigger club, take the bigger wages and the louder crowds. But it was you who made me realise that to take that offer would mean losing more than I could ever gain.

Yes, I could pull on a Chelsea shirt, or Spurs, or even The Arsenal, but I would never be the same player. Too much of me would be left behind at Dulwich. They are the club that made and shaped me.

Even when I am not wearing the shirt, the badge is still tattooed deep in me – it is not something I could remove, even if I wished to.

So I have stayed at Dulwich Hamlet. And the second I made that decision, I was back to my best on the pitch, and my happiness returned. Every time I run out of the tunnel at Champion Hill, I feel like the luckiest and richest man on the planet. I reached 300 goals for the club this season, but the real reward comes from the crowd – they sing my name every week. They are my club. Like you, I will have only one. I know now that this is enough, thanks to you.

This brings me to the final point of my letter.

I would like to repay you, both for your advice and your friendship. I have spoken to Mr Morath, the secretary at Dulwich, and we have agreed we would like to celebrate your career with a friendly match – a testimonial.

We would be happy to travel to Germany for it, if you want to choose a place, or maybe we could play somewhere in between our two cities. (But perhaps not halfway as it would mean playing in the North Sea!) Wherever we decide, we can celebrate your life with Altona and further deepen the ties between our two clubs.

I hope you will not be embarrassed by this offer but flattered. I can think of nothing better than to celebrate your career with one final game. (Which we will win of course ... Ha ha!)

I will look forward to hearing from you, and until then I remain your friend.

Edgar

16

Adi watches Edgar shake his head in wonder as he holds the letter and traces his index finger over the signature he'd written all those years ago. Adi feels almost guilty for watching, and as Edgar looks up he pretends to be looking in the shop window.

"Do you know what is amazing?" Edgar calls, waving at Adi to come back. "Your grandfather replied within weeks, and the friendly match happened. It was Dulwich Hamlet versus Altona 93 all over again."

"I know," Adi replies. "I know about this match!" He can't believe that the jigsaw is coming together like this. Adi reaches into his rucksack again, while Edgar talks on, sounding thrilled to have been reminded of this time and place.

"But what you don't know, Adi, is how much it meant to me to play against your grandfather again. It was incredible to be able to celebrate such a great career with another game."

"Look," Adi says, having found what he was looking for. "Look." And he hands Edgar another clipping from a newspaper. This one is from a local paper, but not from London or Hamburg. It's from somewhere very different: a place called Heligoland.

"I did not realise that your letter and this report were connected," Adi goes on. "But now I see that the match you offered did take place! On the island of Heligoland, in the North Sea. I wish very much that I could have been there to see that match."

"You would've loved it, son," Edgar says. "It was the perfect venue, and the only place we could find that was in between London and Hamburg. I'd never been anywhere like it, such a small island – just a big lump of rock really. It had a few dozen houses, a hotel and a handful of pubs, and a football pitch, most importantly of all. Terrible surface for a passing game, but that didn't matter. We weren't there to win at all costs. We were there to give your granddad a party."

"And here it is, written down," Adi says. "The Stadium on the Rock. And a win for Altona this time!"

Edgar laughs as Adi sits down beside him. He holds the piece of newspaper out so they can read the match report together.

17

FRIENDLY FIRE FOR ADOLF

1 May 1938

Altona 2–1 Dulwich Hamlet (Heligoland)

A small but noisy crowd turned out at our "Stadium on the Rock" today to honour one of Germany's footballing greats, Adolf Jäger.

Heligoland was chosen for its position between the cities of London and Hamburg, and proved a splendid venue for this friendly match, despite the pitch's bumpy, potholed surface.

The match was held in honour of Adolf Jäger, Altona and Germany centre forward, who has hung up his boots at the age of forty. Jäger is a fans' favourite, whose goal records will take some beating.

After the match, the striker thanked the fans of both teams and said he was "looking forward to getting on with my business", a tobacco shop in Hamburg, and "spending time with my family".

Jäger also made special mention of one Dulwich Hamlet player – their favourite winger, Edgar Kail, who came up with the idea for the game in the first place.

Kail scored his team's only goal after thirty-seven minutes from close range, with Kurt Voss poking in a scrappy equaliser for Altona.

Strangely, Jäger misfired for the first 80 minutes. Perhaps the emotion of the occasion was too much for him. But in the 81st minute he found himself taking a dubious penalty, which felt planned simply to get the hero on the score sheet. Jäger made no mistake with the penalty, of course, burying the ball in the bottom left corner.

The match was played in an excellent spirit. There is a long and deep friendship between the two clubs, and it showed in the action. Tackles were hard but fair. The terrible playing surface even created a real moment of humour when the Dulwich winger Gatland tripped and fell into a hole on the left wing. Jäger, ever the gentleman, offered to run and fetch a ladder to help him out.

On the final whistle, there were many handshakes, embraces and Jäger's speech, emotional for many of those watching.

Tomorrow, in Berlin, another Adolf is due to make a speech. And many fear what Adolf Hitler's words might mean for our small island, the country as a whole, and the world beyond that.

If this is to be the last friendly match between our two countries for a while, then we must remember it fondly. For today, on this rock in the middle of the North Sea, real friendship seemed possible.

Attendance: unknown

18

Scotland, 1983

Outside on the bench, Edgar sighs, but Adi can tell it is a sign not of despair but pride. Adi feels pride too. After all, Adolf was his grandfather. His flesh and blood.

The sky is getting darker. Adi looks at the old man beside him and senses something else: a sad quietness creeping over him.

He waits for Edgar to speak, but he says nothing. He is deep in thought. In the end it is too painful for Adi to stay silent.

"Do you think it will rain?" he asks, looking up.

But Edgar doesn't seem to have heard the question. Instead he says, "I couldn't agree more." His voice is quiet, serious. "With the newspaper article, I mean."

"That it was a 'dubious' penalty?" Adi asks. "I am not sure of the word, but I think it means 'dodgy', yes?"

"Yes, it does," Edgar replies. "And it was MORE than dodgy – it was a gift. A goodbye present to your granddad. But I didn't mean the penalty – I meant I agree with the whole article. What it said about Adolf, about what we all felt towards him."

Adi smiles. "It must have been wonderful to be there."

"It was more than wonderful. It was sad, moving, funny – I'd forgotten Gatland fell down the hole! But it was also a difficult day."

The wind is picking up. The old man changes pace with it. "Come on. The weather's turning. Let's get that milk and head home before we get soaked."

As they come out of the shop, Adi wonders why Edgar changed the subject and didn't say anything more about that day. He respects the old man hugely but wants to know what happened next. Adi thinks about how he can help him talk.

Edgar pulls his scarf tighter against the wind and takes Adi's arm as they cross the road. Adi lets him keep hold of it as they head up the hill, but he is surprised at Edgar's pace. He is walking faster than he thought he'd be able to go. But the old man seems keen to get home.

"You see," Edgar explains as they walk on, "the timing of that match was strange. We were there to celebrate your granddad of course, but at the same time we all knew things between our countries were worse than ever. We worried that war was on the way. It was a difficult time. A scary time. We had no way of knowing what was about to happen. But we both knew, deep down, that it would be bad."

"And did you talk about it there?" Adi asks. "Together? Or was it too difficult, with you from England and him from Germany?"

"Oh, we talked about it all right. We might not have known each other all that well, but when we were together, conversation always flowed. Of course, our next chat didn't happen in the bar," Edgar continued. "Not this time. This time, we found each other in our favourite place. Out on the pitch ..."

19

The North Sea was angry, whipping a salty wind across the pitch and into Edgar's face. But he wouldn't be stopped, despite the tiredness in his legs after ninety minutes of football. He had to practise, just like he always did. Thirty minutes practising his crossing to make up for the rubbish ones he'd swung in during the game. It would help relax his muscles too – make his body less stiff and angry in the morning.

The light was fading as Edgar put his first cross in. It was too high, too close to where the keeper would stand to cause him any kind of danger. Edgar frowned and forced his legs into a trot to fetch the ball, scattering the hundreds of seagulls that were pecking at the trampled grass for worms.

After ten minutes, his crosses were no better. So he dug deep and found a new rhythm, which saw the ball fight the wind and win, hitting the six-yard line once, twice, three times in a row. Edgar smiled. One more and he could go inside to bathe and change.

He knew the second he hit the next ball that the contact was perfect. It was getting late and he could barely see the penalty box any more, even from the wing, but he knew the ball would land exactly where he wanted it.

But the ball never bounced, as out of the shadows walked a figure with legs much stiffer than Edgar's. The ball curled towards the man, who never broke stride or even attempted to run towards it, yet it was clear both the ball and he were moving in perfect symmetry.

At that moment, despite the darkening sky, Edgar knew who the figure was – and he knew where the ball would end up.

But the ball made no contact with the man's foot or head. It did not end up in the goal. Instead, the man caught it easily, with a smile.

Edgar found it difficult to find joy in this.

"What are you doing, Adolf?" he said, running towards him. "That's the best cross I've hit all day. You should've headed it home!"

"I am retired," Adolf replied, matter-of-factly, a statement that saddened Edgar even further. "And besides, look how heading the ball has cost me my hair. Let an old man protect what he has left, yes?"

Edgar managed a grin, though Adolf had still made him feel sad. Bald or not, Adolf was too good to not be playing any more.

"So that really is it then?" Edgar asked.

"Of course," Adolf said. "My legs are too tired, and my back is too sore to stock the shop's shelves for three days after a game. Nothing on the shelves means no money in the till. No money in the till means nothing on my kitchen shelves at home. Then how popular will I be?"

There wasn't a lot Edgar could say to that. But without Adolf on the pitch, all he could see was a huge hole at the heart of Altona 93 and an equally big hole in the penalty box.

"So you have no regrets?" asked Edgar. "No what ifs? What if you'd said yes to Munich or Juventus?"

"Not one," Adolf replied. "I have *so* many memories that they have caused this baldness.

They push out of my brain and force the hair from my head!" Then his tone changed, becoming more serious. "How can I have regrets, hmm? Every memory I have on the pitch belongs to either Altona or my country. No one else. I share it with them alone. That makes each memory, to me, so special. You of all people can understand that, I'm sure."

Edgar nodded. Of course he did. He felt the same. "It just makes me sad that the next time our clubs play each other, only one of us will be playing."

"My friend," Adolf said, "by the time our teams play next, with everything else going on in the world, maybe *neither* of us will be playing."

Edgar felt a fear rise in him. It was a fear he felt far too often these days, whenever he turned on the wireless or read the newspaper.

"Do you think it will happen then, Adolf?" Edgar asked. "Do you think war is coming?"

Adolf shook his head sadly, looking much older than his years. "That is not a question I can answer. I am just a shopkeeper – I'm not even a footballer any more. What I know is that there are people in my country who are very, very scared of what lies ahead. But there are also people who believe every word that comes out of Hitler's mouth. Why, I do not know. All Hitler wants us to do is turn our backs on each other, make our friends our enemies. What good can that possibly do, except make all of us afraid? I am scared that soon, if this continues, then it will be too late to turn back, and something other than footballs will be falling out of the sky."

His words fell on Edgar with a great weight, squeezing the air from his lungs and causing his legs to shake.

"It doesn't make sense, Adolf," Edgar said. "And it doesn't matter how many people try to explain it to me. I just can't understand it. War would change everything, get in the way of everything."

"I know. I understand so very little, like you. But I do know that war, any war, cannot last forever, and that while it will build walls for a while, every wall can still be climbed or knocked down in time."

Adolf smiled a sad smile and added, "We are friends. Our clubs are friends, and it will take much more than one man in Berlin to change this for ever."

He fiddled with the lapel of his suit and removed from it a small metal badge shaped in the crest of Altona 93. He pointed to a similar badge on Edgar's training top and said, "We cannot control what happens next, but we can promise that at the end of war, should it arrive, that we will meet again – here, on Heligoland. Until then, perhaps we should swap badges. I will carry Dulwich Hamlet and you carry Altona 93 with you. When we meet again, we will give the badges back and the friendship continues."

Adolf pinned his badge to Edgar's chest and waited as his friend's shaking fingers removed his own and did the same.

Adolf placed his hands firmly on Edgar's shoulders, looking to console the younger man.

"Do not worry, Edgar, my friend. We will meet again, in time, I promise you."

Edgar nodded, blinking back tears as he returned the embrace. "We must, Adolf. We must."

20

Scotland, 1983

Adi leads Edgar up the hill, arm in arm, feeling the wind in his face. It makes his eyes water, and he sees Edgar's do the same. The old man takes out his handkerchief and wipes his eyes.

"You know, that chat your grandfather and I had after the match was very important to me," Edgar says, above the noise of the wind. "I thought of it a thousand times over the months and years that followed. And it helped me. I hoped it helped your granddad too."

"Maybe it gave you both something to look forward to, when the war did take over?" Adi says.

"It did," Edgar replies. "But it was still tough. That night we got on separate boats and went our separate ways – me with the Dulwich lads back to London, and Adolf and his Altona mates to Hamburg. Despite the deal we'd made, there was nothing we could do to stop the war. It was coming."

They push up the hill for a moment, then Adi asks the question he feels he has to: "Did you fight?"

It's a simple question, one that Edgar could answer with one word, but he doesn't reply quickly.

His pause makes Adi ask the question again, in case his English had been too poor to understand.

"In the war, I mean? Did you fight?"

"No," Edgar replies. "I didn't even get to choose. In the first war – the Great War they called it – I was too young. By the second war, I don't know, maybe they thought I was too old? Did you know they called up single men first? Anyway, I still waited every day for the letter summoning me to fight, but it never arrived. I didn't know whether to feel relieved that they never called me up or guilty. It seemed everyone else was being shipped out – all those young, innocent lads – and in the end I wasn't picked. I was on the sub's bench, I suppose. So I worked as a reserve for the police force as well as for the drinks company. Football carried on in a way, but the crowds were small. People had other things to think about. I was getting near the end of my playing days too. And most of the Dulwich team were away fighting."

Edgar slows down again and says, "Eric Pierce, Ron Ebsworth, Reggie Anderson, Billie Parr." He lists the names quietly.

"Sorry, who are they?" Adi asks.

"Young Dulwich players who lost their lives in the war. Heroes, all of them. I should've been fighting alongside them, like we did on the pitch every Saturday."

Edgar and Adi are now passing the park where the local kids are still playing, even though it's raining and getting too dark to see the ball. One of them gives them a wave that seems friendly. Edgar waves back.

"I was left on my own to kick a ball around the park to try to keep fit," Edgar says. "Had to be strong for my wife, Rene. She was quite poorly by then. She had an illness passed down to her from her family."

Adi doesn't respond.

"Are you listening to me?" Edgar asks, suddenly cross, like he was when he first opened the door.

"Yes, sorry," Adi says. "It is just you made me think of my family. We also had illness passed down. Adolf's wife, my grandmother, lived her life not knowing she had a heart disease. She died far too young, when my father was only just a man."

Edgar looks sad. "I had no idea. Your granddad and I had very little time to talk about family in any depth. I'm sorry, son. But you're OK, aren't you? You don't carry the illness too?"

"No," Adi says. "I am fine, thank you."

"Thank goodness for that!"

They've reached the house, and at the front door, Edgar asks, "What did Adolf do in the war? Do you know?"

"My father told me he was not fit enough to fight," Adi explains. "Too many old injuries. So he stayed in Hamburg and worked clearing bombs away. There were so many bombs. Lots that had not exploded."

Adi is dreading the next question – he doesn't know how to give Edgar the answer without upsetting him. Luckily, the old man jumps in.

"It must have been terrifying, doing such a dangerous job." Edgar fumbles with his keys. His hands are cold, so Adi takes over and lets them in.

Edgar goes on, "It was impossible to stay in touch during the war. Everything was muddled, and it was hard to know what was really happening in Germany. You never knew if what the papers said was true or whether they were just trying to keep our spirits up." Edgar sighs at the memory. "Put the milk in the fridge for me, will you?"

Adi does as he is told, and Edgar busies himself looking for something in the shoebox.

Adi comes back into the living room to find Edgar waving an old envelope, never sealed.

"Here you go, look," Edgar says. "I knew I still had it. A letter to your granddad. I wrote it in 1942."

Adi is pleased, of course. Pleased because he wants to know more, but pleased too because it delays him from telling Edgar about what happened to Adolf next.

"I didn't know if I would be allowed to send it," adds Edgar. "It was frowned on, a letter from an Englishman to a German. They probably thought people would let slip what Churchill was planning, as if I knew. So it was never posted, and your granddad never read it."

Adi smiles. "But you kept it."

"I did. And I'll tell you something, I'm glad I wrote it. It helped me. I know it might sound silly, son, but I could read it to you now. If you liked?"

Adi nodded. He wanted to hear more. Of course he did.

21

29 April 1942

Dear Adolf,

This letter might take you by surprise, if it arrives at all.

Who knows, someone in the police may stop it, read it and decide it is so boring that it doesn't deserve the price of the stamp!

Either way, it felt important to try to say hello, Adolf.

You must forgive me, but it seems strange using that name now, with everything that's going on. How does it sit with you, sharing your name with Hitler? I honestly don't know how it would make me feel, but I think we are both too old to think about taking on new names now!

It struck me the other day that, whenever we meet, we are always on opposite sides – now more than ever. I cycle through Dulwich Park most days and yesterday I found myself daydreaming that one day, just once, we might play for the same team. Silly, eh?

I hope you and your family are bearing up. I've seen reports in the newspaper about bombings right across Hamburg and know from what is happening here how scary those nights are. It feels as if they will never end, that you are only inches away from a bomb, even when it lands a mile away.

I wanted you to know that you are in mine and Rene's prayers, for all the good they might do.

I don't know about you, but with all this craziness going on I'm finding it hard to believe in any kind of God. What sort of person would allow this to happen? To leave so many people dead, to make those left behind too scared to go to sleep?

*I don't know what to think any more,
particularly about my part in it. We're
being told all the time that everyone has a
part to play. But I don't know what mine is.
I don't know what position I'm playing.*

*It would be easier if I had a decision
to make – to fight or not to fight. But I
haven't been called up yet, and that makes
it worse. Still, I'm doing what I can, here in
London, working for the Police Reserves.*

*Last Wednesday we had a very near
miss. We were helping people into shelters
during a raid, when a strike hit the very
next street! Too close for comfort. It
scared some of the lads, of course. But me?
I just felt numb. I mean, how can I feel like
that? It's not because I'm brave. I'm as
scared as everyone else. Maybe the numb
feeling just comes from the confusion –
about how we've come to this point and
what will happen next.*

*We've a saying here that sums it up:
feeling like a "fish out of water". I don't
know what you would say in German.
It would be good to be able to ask you.*

About this and other things too. Not least football. I miss it. Don't you?

Anyway, I must go now. I'm on patrol tonight and I have to check on Rene first. She's not well, and I'm really worried that she's not getting better. I don't know what I'd do without her. We keep our minds off her illness by talking about what we'll do after the war, the places we'll see. We've even talked about moving to Scotland. She has family up there still. Could you imagine me in a kilt?! Still, I won't trouble you with the thought of that, if you even know what a kilt is?

I look forward to sending in a cross for you to head home sometime soon, but I don't know when or how that will happen.

I await the day when all this changes.

With my best wishes,
Your good friend, Edgar

22

Scotland, 1983

"Your good friend, Edgar," the old man says,
repeating the last line. Edgar's voice cracked the
first time he tried to say it.

His voice cracked another time, when he read
about Rene's illness, but apart from that he got
through the letter. Just. Adi has been listening as
hard as he can to Edgar. He wants to hear every
detail, hoping that his language skills don't let him
down.

Adi doesn't say anything. He feels like he
might cry if he does. Not because of what he's just
heard but because of what he knows he must say
next.

Edgar breathes out and seems calmer now that
he has delivered the letter at last, despite being

over forty years late. Adi is not Adolf, but he is the next best thing.

"It would mean so much to my grandfather to get this letter in the post," Adi says. "I never met him, so it might sound strange for me to say, but from talking to you today, I feel like I know him a little now. I know that this letter would have made him so very happy."

"Thank you, son," Edgar says. "That means a lot. You're a good lad. Honest. Adolf would've been proud of you, I know that. So, look here …" Edgar puts the note back in its envelope and hands it over. "Consider the letter delivered. Finally."

"Thank you."

Adi keeps hold of the letter and starts to explain. "I know also that my grandfather found the wartime very difficult. The people of Hamburg had to take so much bombing from the sky. His son – my father – was still just a young boy and had to move away to live somewhere more safe. My grandfather's Altona 93 friends were sent to fight. Like your Dulwich friends. And Adolf was left behind at home to do the work that had to be done."

"Just like me," says Edgar. "We were very alike, your granddad and me. Apart from his hair of course!" he adds, smiling half a smile.

"Oh, and by the way," Adi says with a brighter voice, "I don't know if my grandfather knew what a kilt is, but I do!"

Adi has lightened the mood on purpose, to give himself time to prepare for the next step. But as he takes a deep breath, he knows there is no easy way to tell Edgar what happened next. What happened to his grandfather ...

23

Adolf took one step forward, his heavy boots rubbing at the blister on his heel.

He was at the fish market, where Altona meets the docks and the River Elbe. But now there was little of the market left, only burnt timber and rubble.

He wore his bomb sweeper's jacket, but it was too heavy, even for a wintry day like this. Adolf had been picking through the rubble since early morning, searching for anything that might not have exploded yet. The fin of a bomb, the pin of a grenade. He moved bricks carefully, cursing the rats that ran around like they owned the place.

Adolf was tired, but the work had to be done. So he pushed on. He took another single step forward.

Last night had been nothing like the bombing that Hamburg had suffered last July, when there had been several days and nights of anger pouring down from the skies and over 40,000 people killed. But yesterday's attack had been heavy enough to create a serious amount of debris to clamber through.

Adolf's legs were aching. But his heart ached more.

Some days, the end of the war seemed almost in sight, but it did not help ease the pain that Adolf felt. There had been so many unnecessary deaths – those of team-mates, relatives, friends and neighbours.

He swallowed his pain, took another step forward and checked the ground once more. How he hated bomb sweeping – the fear he felt that the next step he took might be his last.

Life used to be so much simpler. Playing football had been noisy, but the noise came from people singing in the stands, not from bombs. If he thought hard enough, he could still hear the fans, making his heart pound proudly.

A-Adolf!
There's only one Adolf.
There's only one Adolf ...

He took one more step forward and let himself smile, but not for long, as he remembered he wasn't the only Adolf any more. There was another Adolf that many people sang for, but he was both dangerous and responsible for this mess.

Adolf Jäger did not like Adolf Hitler – he wanted him out of his head. So he tried to replace him with another song, humming the first thing he could pull from his memory.

Da-da-daa, da-da-daa, de-de-da-daa ...

It was a habit he had, which really annoyed his wife.

"You're doing it again!" she'd say. "Either know the words to the songs you are singing or put a sock in it!"

What a woman she was. His wife had watched more of Adolf's matches than he could count over the years, and had she complained? No, she had not. So when Adolf retired from football, it should have meant happier times for her, more time for them to be together.

But then the other Adolf had to go and spoil it, didn't he, with his war?

It made him so sad. Made him want to go home and be with his wife, but at that moment the best he could do was take his wallet from his jacket and slip out a photo. He always carried it with him, the picture of the two of them in the clubhouse bar after he'd scored his first hat-trick.

His wife was very beautiful, and he looked so young!

Adolf smiled at the strangeness of it. He was not a great striker any more but, of all things, a *defender* of sorts.

Adolf Jäger, of the Bomb Disposal and Defence Unit.

He knew it was a good thing he was doing, an important job, keeping people safe. But he missed how simple life had been as a footballer. Put the ball in the net – that was his job, and he could do that. He did it very well. But not any more.

Adolf felt something kick him in the chest. It was joy at the memory and pain at the loss, it left him confused and dizzy to feel both at the same time.

He went to slide the photograph away, but something else slipped from the other side of his wallet, something small and shiny.

It made the faintest *tinkle* amongst the rubble.

Adolf swore as his eyes searched around his feet for a glint of what had just fallen. Luckily he saw it resting on the edge of a wooden post. It was a miracle it hadn't slipped out of sight for ever, he thought. It was so small but so precious.

He took one step forward and bent down to pick it up. It had been pinned to the inside of his wallet since war had broken out. A small pin badge with the pink and blue crest of Dulwich Hamlet FC.

Edgar's badge.

Adolf remembered the chats they'd had, which he'd always enjoyed. The moment they'd first introduced themselves in the tunnel at the Altona stadium. On the pock-marked pitch on Heligoland. In the bar at Wembley Stadium, where he'd offered Edgar advice over a beer – a rubbish beer compared to what they served here.

Adolf remembered what he'd said to Edgar that day.

I already have so much. I have my shop. I have my family. And I have nights like this.

He could hear himself saying it. He looked forward to more conversations with Edgar. They'd made a promise, hadn't they? To meet on Heligoland again. All they had to do was get through this ... this mess.

What else had he said to Edgar? Oh yes.

One bad tackle, one lunge from a clumsy defender ... One moment, my friend, and it could all be over.

So true, Adolf thought. More true than ever.

He pinned the Dulwich Hamlet badge to his jacket collar, lit a cigarette and went back to the job in hand. He took one step forward and started half-singing again, louder this time. The same tune:

Da-da-daa, da-da-daa, de-de-da-daa ...

And then, from nowhere, the words came back to him. The ones that belonged to the tune:

Da-da-daa, da-da-daa, da-daa ...
Edgar Kail in my heart, keep me Dulwich.
Keep me Dulwich till my dying day.

Adolf allowed himself a smile, sucked again on his cigarette, and took one more step forward.

And in an instant, the ground exploded beneath his feet.

24

Scotland, 1983

Edgar is shaking as Adi finishes the story. He holds
on to the arm of the chair, his hand over the badge
still resting there.

"I'm sorry. Are you OK?" Adi asks. He is on his
feet, heart pounding.

"Yes, thanks, son. I'm OK."

"I didn't want to upset you," Adi goes on. "I
didn't know how to explain what happened in the
end – what little we know. There was nobody
else there, but they could guess what it was. An
unexploded bomb. My grandfather's body was
found, and the badge ... the badge was pinned to
his jacket, just like he said it might be in the letter.
The letter my father was given after Adolf's death."

Edgar slumps back into his chair. His hand is still gripping the badge, but it looks like the rest of his body has given up.

"I always worried deep down that the war might have cost Adolf his life," Edgar says, close to tears. "But I didn't want to believe it. That's why I tried to contact him so many times after the war finished. Five telegrams I sent, but each time no reply. I didn't know whether they'd even been delivered, never mind read. Adolf could've moved house, the house could've been bombed. I didn't know, did I? I didn't know anything! It was still a mess, even after the war ended!"

Edgar tries to stand up, but his body won't let him, and nor will Adi. A gentle hand on his shoulder tells him to stay sitting, at least for a while.

"I need to tell you this," Edgar says. "I didn't give up. I sent one last telegram," he gasps. "I had to, for my own sanity as much as anything. I can still remember the exact words of it." And he rolls off the message without hesitating:

ADOLF, MY FRIEND – WE WILL MEET AS PLANNED ON HELIGOLAND – TO SWAP BADGES BACK – SATURDAY 16 OCT 3PM? –

I WILL BE THERE – SPORTING WISHES –
EDGAR KAIL – STOP

He might be sitting down, but Edgar is still breathless, his eyes desperate. "I did go back there," Edgar goes on. "I kept my promise. I had to."

25

Heligoland, 16 October 1948

Edgar liked the feeling of sand under his feet. It had been a rough crossing to Heligoland, enough to turn his face green. But as he stepped off the boat his normal colour returned. He was heading to the Stadium on the Rock, not that it had ever really *been* a stadium, more a rough, potholed pitch with a sandy running track around it. Thick stone steps were cut into the rock on one side for terraces and on the other side there was nothing but a shallow cliff and then the sea. But still, Edgar loved the place and what had happened there before.

The journey here had taken it out of him. He was nowhere near as fit as he used to be. Still, there was a spring in his step that day that he hadn't felt for a very long time.

Hadn't felt since before his wife Rene had died. And before that, when he last played for Dulwich.

Edgar's football career was over. He had played on during the war, but matches were rare and the standard was low, with so many good players away fighting. The one positive thing was that the women's game had stepped up and was thriving, but by the time the men started to return home, Edgar's playing days were over.

Rene had passed away in March the previous year, after battling more bravely than Edgar could ever have done. He was with her then, holding her hand. He'd sung her a music-hall song that she loved until she closed her eyes that final time.

Edgar had felt like giving up but knew he couldn't. He threw himself into sorting everything out. It helped with the grief a little. The funeral, the will, then the sale of the house in Dulwich and the move north to Scotland.

But one thing still needed doing. One thing as important as everything else.

If Adolf *could* keep the promise they'd made, Edgar knew he would be there, waiting on Heligoland. They'd shaken on it. So after sending that one last telegram to Adolf, Edgar took a risk:

he bought a ticket for the boat and now here he was.

He hoped he might also see someone involved with the last friendly match, anyone who might be able to fill in some of the gaps of the last ten years. But when Edgar reached the ground, all he found was a howling wind.

He walked out to the centre circle. A seagull swooshed past his head, making him jump with alarm. Sadly, the bird was the only other form of life there.

Edgar felt surprised and sad. He'd been certain Adolf would make it.

If seagulls could laugh, this one was in stitches as it rested on top of a snapped corner flag leaning in the wind. But it wasn't the bird Edgar was most interested in. He'd spotted something next to it: a brown lump of leather that used to be a ball.

He gave it a prod. It was fairly flat but still kickable. Better than nothing.

Edgar stared at it for a moment, like he'd forgotten what to do with it.

Then he prepared himself. He slowly took one step back, then another.

The seagull took off, alarmed.

Edgar looked down at his shoes – brown leather lace-ups, no grip and useless for football. Then with two quick jogs on the spot, he looked to the penalty area, to where he wanted the ball to drop.

Caw! Caw! Caw! The seagull had landed on the crossbar, and Edgar had become seventeen years old again, in his mind at least. He swung in a fantastic cross with perfect pace, perfect flight, soaring in the North Sea air ... It invited a striker to arrive between the penalty spot and six-yard box just as it curled away from the invisible keeper's grasp.

Adolf, where are you? Edgar thought, his eyes wide and hopeful.

Caw! Caw! Caw! Even the seagull was calling for the great German striker.

Edgar felt a rush of blood to the heart. A surge of something. Suddenly, he was totally happy.

But there was no one there to meet his cross. No header. No volley. No *BOOM* – somewhere between a kiss and a punch.

No Adolf.

Edgar felt crushed, and silly. For some reason he'd hoped – no, *believed* – that if he sent in a good enough cross, then Adolf would appear. Just like he'd done that night before their first match: a blur of black, white and red hoops, leaping to meet Edgar's cross as if from nowhere.

Was it too much to ask? After all, it had happened on this very pitch! OK, so Adolf had caught the ball that day. But still, he had been there.

But not today. There was no Adolf.

The flat, shapeless ball landed on the other side of the six-yard box and rolled towards the edge of the pitch. It kept going. And going. Until it ran off the edge and into the sea.

Edgar looked down at his filthy shoes and at the rocky pitch below them. He felt old. He smiled a sad smile. Then he started to cry and didn't know how to stop.

26

Scotland, 1983

In the living room, Edgar is crying. Adi doesn't
like to see this but isn't sure what to do about it.
Should he move closer to him? Put an arm around
his shoulder? Adi doesn't want to make the old
man feel worse.

"I'm sorry that my grandfather was not there
to meet you," he says, and Edgar looks at him with
wide red eyes.

"That's hardly your fault, son, is it?"

"Well, no," Adi says. "But from what you
tell me, I know Adolf would have been so happy
to be there, to see you. I do not think that your
telegrams ever reached his home." Adi holds
up the envelope. "They were not in my folder, I
promise you. And from what my father tells me
and from what I read in books, Germany after

the war was completely destroyed. In ruins. Everything needed rebuilding, so little food. I am not surprised that telegrams went missing."

"It was the same here," Edgar says. "We might have won the war, but it often didn't feel like it. Too many deaths, too many towns and cities blown to pieces. That was one of the reasons I left London."

Tears well in Edgar's eyes again. "I felt guilty you know, for leaving. I should've stuck around and rolled my sleeves up, done my bit to rebuild London like everyone else did. But I couldn't. Every street corner I turned, I expected to see Rene, and every time she wasn't there it hurt me. It was like a thousand deaths every day.

"At first, I threw myself back into the football. Not playing – my legs had gone – but coaching the kids. But after that second trip to Heligoland, I couldn't even be around Dulwich Hamlet. It reminded me too much of what I'd had and lost. I had enough grief in my life – I couldn't deal with any more. I just wanted to forget."

Adi breathes out and slumps slightly in his chair. He has met so few people who actually lived during the war and even fewer that wanted to talk about it. As a result, Adi hasn't ever really thought about what happened when the fighting stopped. He presumed people in England would be happy – they'd won, after all? But now he feels foolish for not realising that they would be in pain too.

"You know," Adi says, "I do understand what you are saying. About forgetting. This mission that I am on, to bring this badge back to you, it should not have been mine to carry out."

"What do you mean?" Edgar asks.

"The letter Adolf wrote was for my father," Adi continues. "It should have been him finding you, many, many years ago. But of course my father was still only a boy then. It was not like he could just travel around Europe to find you. And from what my father told me, it would have been impossible to. Everything was still so crazy. He never had the chance, like I do now. Maybe the badge also reminded him of the past, and that caused him too much pain. So my father buried it in this envelope, in a drawer. It stayed there until he found it again and passed it to me. I am sorry it has taken so long."

But Edgar, it seems, is not having any of Adi's guilt. Instead, he picks the badge up carefully from the arm of the chair like it is the world's most precious jewel.

"Some things, son, are worth waiting for," Edgar says. "It doesn't matter to me how long it took you to get here. I'd have waited till the day I died to see this badge again. What matters is that you found me. You found me, and you've brought me back to life. Me and your granddad."

Adi smiles. His mission is complete. Well, almost.

He leans forward and, with permission, takes the badge from Edgar's hands. Adi pins it to the old man's cardigan and more tears escape from Edgar's eyes.

"Please," Adi says. "There is no need to cry. I am happy. My grandfather, he will now be happy. So you will be happy too."

Edgar sobs a happy sob, and his shaking hands fumble at his scarf.

"Then I need to keep my end of the bargain too," he says. "The deal was that we'd meet after the war and swap badges back."

Edgar moves his scarf to reveal a hidden badge of his own: an Altona 93 crest. It's the black, white and red that Adi knows and loves so well. The badge is old but cared for.

"It rarely leaves my cardigan, this badge," Edgar says. "Though it has been in the washing machine a few times."

His fingers try to remove it, but every attempt seems useless.

"Nothing works any more," Edgar says. He sounds frustrated.

"Please," says Adi gently, "please, leave it. There is no need to take it off."

"There's every need," Edgar disagrees. "That was the deal. It was a loan, a swap. You need to take this badge with you."

Adi shakes his head. "Please, Edgar. There is no need. My grandfather is gone. I think he would be very happy to see the two badges carried together by you. It is much, much better this way. It is perfect, in fact."

Edgar admits defeat for a moment, beaten by both his own fingers and the boy's will. But then he leaps up suddenly, making Adi jump. "Wait here!" Edgar says. He moves with speed, limping from the room, leaving Adi alone.

He is gone longer than Adi expects. Adi looks at every corner of the room again and thinks about how modest Edgar is. Apart from his shoebox, there is no sign of his footballing life anywhere.

Edgar has been gone too long, and Adi grows concerned. He panics when there is a thud above him, but then he hears a curse, followed by the plod of stiff legs finding their way down the stairs.

Edgar returns with sweat on his forehead and a smile on his face. It suits him. Makes him look years younger.

In his hand is an odd-shaped lump of old brown leather.

"It didn't take me long to find this," Edgar says. "I knew where it was. Same place it's been forever, on the chest of drawers opposite my bed. It was the bloody pump I was looking for. I didn't want to show you it when it was flat."

Edgar holds it up. It is a football. Adi touches it. The leather feels hard, almost brittle. He doesn't want to think about how heavy and painful it would be to head.

Adi looks at it more carefully, and his eyes fall on two faded scrawls etched into the leather skin.

"This is the match ball from the first time I met your granddad," Edgar explains. "April 1925. A lifetime ago now. Actually, it was the second time I met him, but the first time I played *against* him." Edgar suddenly looks shy, embarrassed. "You know, the night I managed the hat-trick."

Adi smiles and looks at the signatures. It's hard to believe it's the same ball that his grandfather wrote on. He wants to stare at it for hours.

"I cannot believe you still have it!" Adi says. "You should put it down here, on display, for everyone to see!"

Edgar is shocked by the idea. "Oh no!" he says. "I couldn't possibly do that."

"Why not?" Adi asks.

"Because the ball is yours now."

"What? No, I couldn't!"

Edgar shakes his head and smiles widely. "I insist. It's only right. I've no one else to pass it on to. No one who'd want it. And besides, you brought me *this*." His fingers trace the outline of the badge on his cardigan.

Adi looks at his grandfather's name on the ball – at the way he has looped the g in the surname. Adi writes his g's exactly like that.

He doesn't know what to say, or how to simply say yes. In the end Edgar doesn't give Adi the chance.

"Actually, there is one condition to you taking the ball," Edgar says.

Adi looks at him. What could it be?

From his shoebox, Edgar pulls a pen.

"Before you take it, you must sign it too."

Adi looks at him, horrified. "What? No. No way." He waves a hand in front of his face in case his English has let him down. "I can't do that. This ball is precious. It is about you and my grandfather."

Edgar takes a second, a heartbeat, to think about his answer. "You're almost right," he says. "It *was* about us. But now there are three people in this story: Adolf, Edgar ... and you."

Again, Adi doesn't know what to say but realises Edgar will not take no for an answer. So as Edgar holds the ball, Adi slowly presses the pen onto the leather, beside the two faded names.

Adi writes slowly, carefully, not wanting to mess it up. And when Edgar sees what he has written, he gasps.

"I've just realised I've never even asked you what your name is," Edgar says. "What a silly old fool." This makes Adi laugh.

Edgar stands and offers Adi his hand in friendship. Adi accepts it.

"I am so glad you found me," Edgar says. "And your name could not be more perfect. You are clearly your own person, but you are also *so* like him. Brave, adventurous and honest. Thank you, Adi Jäger."

And Kail passes the ball to Jäger perfectly, just as he did on their first meeting, so many years ago.

Authors' Note

Edgar Kail and Adolf Jäger were real people: talented, much-loved footballers. They hung up their boots many years ago, but they are not forgotten. Today the road that leads to the Dulwich Hamlet stadium is called Edgar Kail Way, and the stadium where Altona 93 play is named after Adolf Jäger.

At every Dulwich match, home or away, the fans still sing for Edgar. His face is on badges pinned to supporters' hats, and both he and Adolf appear in fanzines and on stickers.

You might think this isn't very remarkable, but remember, these teams aren't Manchester United or Bayern Munich – they are two non-league teams that play football five or six divisions beneath the top leagues.

On top of that, it's nearly one hundred years since Edgar or Adolf played for their clubs, but *still* these two men are celebrated by the fans. They are also loved by the two of us, Phil and Waggy. It was after Phil spotted a badge on Waggy's hat that we became fascinated by them and by the real friendship that exists between Dulwich Hamlet and Altona 93.

We started to ask each other questions, as writers tend to do:

Do you think Edgar and Adolf knew each other well? Did they become friends?

Did Adolf give young Edgar advice on his career?

And what about the war? Did Edgar and Adolf keep in touch despite the conflict between England and Germany?

We couldn't find the REAL answers to these questions, so again, we did what writers do: we asked each other the question "What if?" We began to make up a story with our own answers – a fictional account of what their relationship MIGHT have been.

So this is not a biography. It's not an account of Edgar and Adolf's real lives, but something different, something imaginative. We hope it might bring them and the period they lived in to life for you.

We've tried to include some facts about them that ARE true: the real Edgar *did* play for England three times (and was the last non-league player to do so – imagine that!). The real Edgar *was* a drinks salesman, and Adolf *did* own a tobacco shop.

We felt details like this – and the fact that footballers back then drank and smoked (can you believe that?) – were important. They help to bring the characters back to life and reveal truths about the time in which the story is set.

There are events in the story that are pure fiction, of course. For example, we've changed the years in which they were born and their family situations. The Edgar in this book is still alive in 1983 whereas the real Edgar wasn't (he died in 1976). We invented the match between England and Germany at Wembley and made up Adolf's testimonial on Heligoland. However, the match between Altona and Dulwich in 1925 really did happen, and that really *was* the score.

What mattered to us was that we were writing a book about friendship – one that is unbreakable, no matter what happens. This became even more important as the writing went on.

You see, the two of us are old friends.

We met nearly thirty years ago and have remained close pals ever since. We've experienced ups and downs – sometimes laughing, sometimes crying together, and often playing football. (In our younger days, Phil had a "good engine" and Waggy could "pick a pass" – you can work out whether THAT is fact or fiction!)

So when we decided to write a book together, it wasn't a surprise that we were drawn to tell a story about *friendship* – one that was rooted in football but which went WAY beyond that.

We really do hope you've enjoyed meeting both Edgar and Adolf – that you can see why they became heroes to us. We hope that, like us, you'll carry them with you wherever you go.

Most of all, we hope you enjoyed reading it as much as we enjoyed writing it together.

Phil & Waggy

Author spotlight

Authors Michael Wagg (Waggy) and Phil Earle have been friends for nearly thirty years, having met at Hull University where they were studying Drama. They forged their footballing friendship playing for the Shakesperoes and went on together to form the Penge Institute of Soccer Skills.

Waggy is a writer, actor and Dulwich Hamlet fan who lives in south London. He has written for the *Guardian* and the *Observer*, and writes regularly for the theatre. He is also the author of the non-fiction football book *The Turning Season*.

Phil lives in Yorkshire and supports the mighty Hull City, but Waggy doesn't hold that against him! He is the award-winning author of fifteen books for children and teenagers, including *Demolition Dad*, *Being Billy* and *Mind the Gap*.

Background to the novel

Dulwich Hamlet FC and Altona 93

Two football clubs play a major role in *Edgar & Adolf*: the English football club Dulwich Hamlet FC, which is based in London, and the German football club Altona 93, which is based in Hamburg. There is a strong bond between the two clubs. Both were formed in 1893, and they first played against each other in 1925 (as you have read in the novel). Dulwich won 4–1.

The result was written in record books, but the link between the two clubs was forgotten for a long time afterwards. Until one day in 2010, when a Dulwich Hamlet supporter called Mishi visited the Altona ground and an Altona 93 supporter called Jan said hello to him. As they chatted, they wondered if their two clubs shared a history and decided to find out. They told other fans about what they discovered, and the two clubs became connected once again, over eighty years later.

Since then there have been supporters' games and a match between the teams in Dulwich (which Altona won 5–3). Then, in 2018, they played against each other again in Hamburg, to celebrate the 125th anniversary of their founding (the score was 4–1 to Dulwich, just like in 1925!). Thanks to Jan and Mishi, new friendships have been formed that continue today.

Football

Football became a very popular sport in the second half of the nineteenth century. The first English football club was Sheffield FC, formed in 1857. The rules of football were finally agreed in 1863, when the Football Association (also known as the FA) was formed. The first FA Cup took place in 1872 with just thirteen clubs competing. However, by the end of the nineteenth century, there were hundreds of professional and amateur football clubs competing from across the United Kingdom. Dulwich Hamlet FC was one of almost thirty football clubs formed in 1893 alone. The German FA was formed in 1900, and the first national championship final was played in 1903 at Altona 93's football ground.

Germany and Britain

Much of the action of *Edgar & Adolf* takes place in the 1920s and 1930s, between the end of the First World War in 1918 and the start of the Second

World War in 1939. Relations were good between Germany and Britain until 1933, when Adolf Hitler came to power as leader of the Nazi party. As Hitler built up the Nazi army, air force and navy, Britain began to see Germany as a threat. By 1938, the year when Edgar and Adolf meet for the last time in the novel, it was predicted by many people that war would take place between Britain and Germany. War was later declared on 3 September 1939.

The authors make a close connection between the story of Edgar and Adolf and the war between their two countries that followed their final meeting. In doing so, the importance of friendship is highlighted, showing that even though countries and governments may disagree and fight, friendship and respect between friends can survive.

There is more about the true stories that inspired Michael Wagg and Phil Earle to write the novel in the authors' note on page 123.

Who's who in this novel

Edgar Kail is an elderly man who lives in Scotland. He is retired but used to work as a drinks salesman. In his youth he played football for Dulwich Hamlet FC in the 1920s and 1930s.

Adi Jäger is a seventeen-year-old boy from Hamburg who has travelled all the way from Germany to Scotland to find Edgar Kail. Adi is the grandson of Adolf Jäger.

Adolf Jäger was Adi's grandfather. He owned a tobacco shop and played football for Altona 93 in Hamburg in the 1920s and 1930s. He and Edgar Kail became friends when their teams played each other in a football match.

What to read next

Divided City by Theresa Breslin

A gripping football tale about two boys who must find their own answers – and their own way forward – in a world divided by differences. This story grabs you and helps you discover the power of friendship in overcoming the influences that can divide us.

When the Guns Fall Silent by James Riordan

A powerful, moving story about one boy's journey through the First World War, of the horrors he faced there, and of the significant moment when, amongst all the bloodshed, the fighting gave way to football on the frozen ground of no man's land.

Armistice Runner by Tom Palmer

The moving story of Lily, who discovers her great-grandfather's diaries from the First World War and learns of his incredible bravery. Can his acts help her to reconnect with her family and inspire her to succeed in her fell-running races?

What do you think?

1. Adi travels from Hamburg to Scotland to see Edgar. Would you have made that long journey to see a friend of your grandfather's? What does this journey tell you about the character of Adi?

2. In the novel, both Edgar and Adolf turn down offers from big professional clubs that would have paid them to play football. Do you think they made the right decision?

3. Read the authors' note on page 123. Are you surprised to discover that Edgar and Adolf were real people, and that some of the events in the story actually happened?

4. Some of the events in the story are made up. Can you think of an event to add to the end of the story that shows the new friendship that has been formed between Edgar and Adi?

Quick quiz

When you have finished reading *Edgar & Adolf*, answer these questions to see how much you can remember about the novel. The answers are on page 137.

1. What is the name of Edgar's football team?

2. What is the name of the ground where Edgar's football team play?

3. What is the name of Adolf's football team?

4. Why has Adi travelled all the way to Scotland to find Edgar?

5. What was Adolf's job during the Second World War?

6. Edgar and Adolf play in a football match on the island of Heligoland. Why was this place chosen for the match?

7. What does Edgar give Adi to take home with him?

Word list

attendance: the number of people at a place or an event

bemused: puzzled, confused

brittle: hard and easily broken or snapped

debut: a first appearance

defender: a player in a sport whose role it is to defend the goal

dubious: doubtful or uncertain

embraced: welcomed or accepted willingly; also hugged

fearless: brave; acting without thinking first

flourish: an exaggerated movement of the hand

fumble: to handle something clumsily

instinctive: based on instinct, not thought or training

jinking: to change direction suddenly, zigzagging

lunge: a sudden movement forward

masterful: extremely skilled and powerful

numb: to have no physical feeling, or have no emotional feeling

occasional: does not happen very often

pock-marked: full of shallow holes

possession: having control of the ball in a sport; also something that is owned

precious: of great value or importance

recognises: to know what something is because you have seen it before

rummage: to look through or search for something

startled: surprised, shocked

summoning: ordering someone to do something or go somewhere

telegram: a message sent through telephone wires, then printed on paper and delivered by hand

terraces: deep, wide steps at a football ground on which spectators used to stand as it was cheaper to stand than to sit to watch the match

testimonial: a written statement highlighting a person's qualities and skills, or sports match held in honour of a player

thriving: growing very successfully

Quick quiz answers

1. Dulwich Hamlet FC

2. Champion Hill

3. Altona 93

4. To return the Dulwich Hamlet badge Edgar
    once gave to Adolf

5. Clearing unexploded bombs

6. Because Heligoland is an island in between
    Great Britain and Germany

7. A leather football signed by both Edgar
    and Adolf

Super-Readable ROLLERCOASTERS

Super-Readable Rollercoasters are an exciting new collection brought to you through a collaboration between Oxford University Press and specialist publisher Barrington Stoke. Written by bestselling and award-winning authors, these titles are intended to engage and enthuse, with themes and issues matched to the readers' age.

The books have been expertly edited to remove any barriers to comprehension and then carefully laid out in Barrington Stoke's dyslexia-friendly font to make them as accessible as possible. Their shorter length allows readers to build confidence and reading stamina while engaging in a gripping, well-told story that will ensure an enjoyable reading experience.

Other titles available in the Super-Readable Rollercoasters series:

Lightning Strike by Tanya Landman
Rat by Patrice Lawrence
I Am The Minotaur by Anthony McGowan
Dark Peak by Marcus Sedgwick

Free online teaching resources accompany all the titles in the Super-Readable Rollercoasters series and are available from:

http://www.oxfordsecondary.com/superreadable